This book is dedicated to
Gilbert for making Ivy's
mum so happy

x x x

EGMONT

First published in paperback in Great Britain 2013
by Jelly Pie, an imprint of Egmont UK Limited
The Yellow Building. 1 Nicholas Road
London W11 4AN

Text copyright © 2013 Kjartan Poskitt
Illustrations copyright © 2013 David Tazzyman

The moral rights of the author and illustrator have been asserted

ISBN 978 1 4052 6574 4

1 3 5 7 9 10 8 6 4 2

www.egmont.co.uk
www.agathaparrot.co.uk

A CIP catalogue record for this title is available from the British Library

Printed and bound by CPI Group (UK) Ltd, Croydon, CR0 4YY

54089/1

FSC MIX Paper FSC® C018306

EGMONT LUCKY COIN

Our story began over a century ago, when seventeen-year-old
Egmont Harald Petersen found a coin in the street.

He was on his way to buy a flyswatter, a small hand-operated
printing machine that he then set up in his tiny apartment.

The coin brought him such good luck that today Egmont has
offices in over 30 countries around the world. And that lucky
coin is still kept at the company's head offices in Denmark.

Agatha Parrot
and the Thirteenth Chicken

Typed out neatly by
Kjartan Poskitt

Illustrated by David Tazzyman

EGMONT

The gang!

When **Bianca** washes her trombone in the bath, she can blow bubbles like footballs!

Martha says she never looks for old crisps down the back of the sofa but she does.

Agatha (that's me).
One time I had my hair
combed for a photo and
nobody knew who I was.
And that's true.

Ivy refuses to eat
cabbage but she can
put spiders in her
mouth!

Ellie is too scared to
play hide and seek, in case
we all forget about her.

ODD STREET

No 1	No 3	No 5	No 7	No 9
Bianca	Martha	Agatha	Ivy	Ellie

SCHOOL

No chickens were hurt during the course of writing this book because chickens are good and we LIKE chickens.

CONTENTS

The Little New Things

· ·

Hiya!

I hope you like books written by somebody who tipped a whole box of cornflakes out over her head. That's me!

1

Don't worry, I'm not completely mad. I had a very good reason for the cornflake thing – I thought a giant ghost chicken had burst out of a lump in the wallpaper. If you were me you'd have done exactly the same, honestly you would! You'll understand why when you've read the story, so let's start at the beginning.

My name is Agatha Jane Parrot and I go to Odd Street School which is at the end of Odd Street where I live. And even though the cornflake thing makes perfect sense, I do have one thing about me that I have to admit is quite embarrassing.

I just LOVE the first day back at school after the holidays.

I know that's weird. School is full of lessons, rules, being quiet, tests, old lady teachers, times tables and freezing cold toilets shiver shiver YUK!

But the reason I can't wait to get

back is that there's always a NEW THING.

Sometimes it's really obvious like when they built a climbing frame in the playground with a slide! It was just so brilliant. EVERYBODY went on it including our new teacher Miss Pingle even though she says she never did. Miss Pingle is well cool because her hair changes colour every week, and we ALL saw her having a quick go when she thought

4

there wasn't anybody watching. She didn't know we were looking out of the library window. She came sliding down waving her hands in the air and went WHEEEE really loud, and we heard her ha ha!

But last term when we went back to school, there wasn't a big new thing like the climbing frame, so me and my friends went round looking for little new things. Here's what the others found and I can tell you that one of them is very important in the story later on! See if you can guess which one it is.

1) Bianca Bayuss noticed that the rubber plant in our class had grown a new leaf. Oooh . . .

Could this be important in the story? Maybe the plant grows more and more leaves and turns the whole school into a jungle with tigers and elephants? Actually it doesn't but it would be good if it did.

2) Martha Swan saw Miss Pingle had got a new bag exactly the same colour as her hair. How cool is that? We had a big argument about what colour

Miss P's bag/hair was. I said
dark red, but Martha said
purple and Bianca said it was
maroon so we asked Miss P.
The answer was *Damson Dream*
so we'd never have got that in a
million years.

3) Ivy Malting spotted that Miss
Wizzit had her ears pierced!
Miss Wizzit is the school
receptionist and her main job
is guarding the photocopier.

She HATES anybody using it, and there's no way she would have left it while she sneaked off to get her ears done. Ivy says that Miss Wizzit probably did it herself with her stapler. Ugh!

Sorry, you'll have to block that thought out. Think about daisies and doughnuts and happy things. La-la la-la lah . . .

4) Ellie Slippin said Motley the caretaker had grown a green moustache! It turns out he'd had a mug of pea soup and some of it had got stuck to his top lip. It's not suprising it fooled us though because it was there for three days until

10

Mrs Twelvetrees* told him.

(* Mrs T is the headteacher.
She's a bit crazy so I bet she
only told Motley about his
green moustache because
she'd got jealous and wanted
one herself ha ha!)

So which new thing do you think
comes into the story? Is it the rubber
plant, the bag, Miss Wizzit's ears

or the green moustache? And what new thing did I find?

If you want to know, keep reading!

The Big New Thing

· ·

I didn't find my new thing until the Monday after we got back. I was going past the reception desk when the door buzzer went. Miss Wizzit pushed a button and spoke into the intercom.

'Wizzit?' asked Miss Wizzit.

'Greetings,' said a voice. 'We are

the Eggs Experience company.'

'Kitchen deliveries go to the kitchen door,' snapped Miss Wizzit.

'It's not for the kitchen,' said the voice. 'The children are going to hatch the eggs out.'

Miss Wizzit pulled the sort of face that you can only pull if you're Miss Wizzit imagining lots of kids sitting on nests full of eggs.

'Don't be silly,' said Miss Wizzit, but then Mrs Twelvetrees came dashing out of her office.

'Is that the egg people?' she gushed, all excited. 'Do let them in Miss Wizzit.'

Egg people? WOW! What a brilliant new thing. It was even better than Motley's green moustache.

The egg people were two men with bushy beards, and they were wearing long hairy dressing gowns and sandals. One of them had an old shopping basket covered in a red

tea-towel, and the other one had a
big plastic box with a wire coming
out of it.

'Here are the fruits of our
feathered community,' said the one
with the basket. He pulled the towel
away to show he had a load of eggs
sitting on some straw.

'And here is the electric mother,'
said the other one.

'The *what*?' said Miss Wizzit.

'It's the incubator to make the

eggs hatch out,' said Mrs Twelvetrees.

The egg people put the eggs and the incubator on the desk, then one of them passed an envelope to Mrs Twelvetrees.

'We leave you in peace,' said the egg people, then they both did a polite little bow and left.

'Aren't the egg people just wonderful?' said Mrs T. 'They live in a cave and grow their own clothes. It's a mystery how they survive!'

'What izzit?' asked Miss Wizzit pointing at the envelope.

Mrs Twelvetrees looked inside.

'It's a bill for five hundred pounds,' she said.

'Mystery solved,' said Miss Wizzit.

Chicken Crazy

It was going to take a day or two for the eggs to hatch, so the incubator was set up in the tiddly tots' class where little old Miss Bunn teaches. You wouldn't think there would be much excitement about a plastic box full of eggs sitting on a table doing nothing, would you?

WRONG!

All the tiddlies went chicken crazy.

To start with, Miss Bunn got them round the plinky plonk piano and taught them one of the greatest songs in the world. You must know it, it goes:

Chick chick chick chick
CHICKEN!
Lay a little egg for me.
Chick chick chick chick

CHICKEN!

I want one for my tea.

(Did you sing that out loud when you read it? If you did then you are a STAR! Have a round of applause clap clap clap.)

On the next day Miss Bunn had all the tiddlies making chicken hats out of yellow paper with orange cardboard beaks. Of course none of the tiddlies could wait for the glue

to dry, so they all put them on

and the hats got stuck to their hair

WICKED!

But that wasn't the best bit. The BEST bit was the massive chicken picture which they drew to cover their classroom door. It was supposed to be one big chicken, but all the tiddlies had taken turns to draw on the wings and legs and other bits. It ended up with seven feet, thirty tiny wings, five beaks (most of them with teeth), three hands, sunglasses, a pirate flag and a flower growing out of its bottom.

Afternoon playtime was crazy. We were all outside surrounded by chicken-headed tiddly tots who were running round and screaming 'Chick chick chick chick **CHICKEN!**'

It was all completely brilliant apart from one thing, and that one thing was called Gwendoline Tutt. Gwendoline is in a different class from us **THANK GOODNESS**. She's the lanky one with the pink bike who lives in the biggest house

25

on Odd Street and she's far too posh for anything.

'Give it a rest!' shouted Gwendoline. 'Honestly! A few eggs and the whole school goes stupid.'

We all know why Gwendoline was in a mood. Gwendoline had wanted the eggs to be in her class and Gwendoline doesn't like it when Gwendoline doesn't get what Gwendoline wants. But if she thought she could spoil the fun, she

was wrong. Miss Bunn came out of the door and called the tiddlies over.

'One of the eggs is moving,' said Miss Bunn.

'Oooooh!' said the tiddlies.

'That means the first chicken is getting ready to come out!' said Miss Bunn.

'CHICK CHICK CHICK CHICK CHICKEN!' shouted the tiddlies.

After playtime, me and Martha

went past Miss Bunn's classroom and looked in the door. All the tiddlies were round the table and Miss Bunn had taken the lid off the incubator.

'Let's see if any chickens can hear me,' said Miss Bunn. She clicked her tongue a few times then said to the eggs, 'Hello little chickens!'

They all listened carefully. Sure enough a little squeaky noise came from one of the eggs! Me and Martha even heard it over by the door.

'That is so cool!' said Martha.

'Would anybody else like to say hello?' asked Miss Bunn.

Immediately every single tiddly screamed at the egg.

'CHICK   CHICK   CHICK CHICK CHICKEN . . .'

The egg went very quiet. I don't blame it. I bet the chicken changed its mind about hatching and decided to stay inside. Imagine being born and the first thing you see are all these giant tiddlies screaming at you with orange beaks growing out of their heads. Scary!

Next morning was Wednesday and as soon as Motley opened the school doors, all the tiddlies charged in still wearing their chicken hats. WAHEY! They ran down the corridor chucking their coats and lunchbags everywhere, then burst into their classroom to see what had happened.

Miss Bunn was staring at a few fluffy blobs in the incubator.

'We've got four so far,' said Miss Bunn.

'OOOOOH!' said the tiddlies.

Nobody in school could concentrate for the whole day. Every so often a huge shout of, 'Chick chick chick chick CHICKEN!' would echo round from Miss Bunn's class

as another chicken appeared. By playtime there were seven chicks, by lunchtime there were eleven, and by afternoon playtime the last two eggs had hatched which made thirteen chicks altogether.

All the other classes took turns to go in and see the chicks in the incubator. When we went in, Miss Bunn was clearing some bits of shell

away. The chicks looked a bit wet from being inside the eggs.

'They need to stay in the incubator tonight,' said Miss Bunn. 'By tomorrow they'll be dried out and fluffy, and then they'll need somewhere bigger to live.'

It all sounded so simple, didn't it?

It wasn't!

Motley's Box of Great Mystery

On Thursday we were all in class when the door burst open and Motley came in walking backwards. He was carrying one end of an old recycling box and big Mrs Potts the dinner lady was carrying the other end. The box had some old chair legs sticking out of the top, and dangling between them was a shiny metal lightshade which was bashing and banging about.

Motley and big Mrs Potts managed to squeeze their way past our chairs without killing anybody, and plonked the whole thing down on the window table.

Motley straightened it up and gave it a wipe with his cloth, then he stood back and grinned at us proudly.

'It's very nice,' said Miss Pingle trying to be nice.

'Yes, it's very nice,' we all said

and then we all went quiet.

Poor old Motley. I think he'd expected us to give him a round of applause. He looked a bit sad.

'Right then,' he said. 'There it is. We'll leave you to it.'

Big Mrs Potts obviously felt sorry for him. 'I thought they'd be pleased,' she said.

'Me too,' said Motley.

They were shuffling their way back to the door when Ivy blurted out, 'What is it?'

'It's a brooding box for the chickens of course,' said Motley. 'It's too big to go in Miss Bunn's class, so they'll have to come in here.'

'WAHOO!' we all cheered and Motley went all smiley.

'Mr Motley has fixed up this heating light,' explained big Mrs Potts. 'It used to hang down over my kitchen worktop to keep the dinners warm.'

'But what if the light makes the chickens too hot?' asked Miss Pingle.

'Mr Motley thought of that,' said big Mrs Potts. 'Didn't you, Mr Motley?'

'Of course,' said Motley. 'That's the clever part of my invention.'

He pointed at the side of the box. There was a switch and next to it was a control knob with numbers round it.

'If you want to make it hotter or colder, you turn this knob,' he said.

'He's so clever,' said big Mrs Potts.

Then big Mrs Potts took Motley off for a cup of tea I expect but I don't know for sure because it's not like I was following them or anything.

The Potato Headed Monster

As soon as we got Motley's box, we wanted to put the chickens in it, but we didn't dare to go and get them from Miss Bunn's class while the tiddlies were watching. There would have been a tiddly riot! That's not funny either, because my sister Tilly is in there, and she says that some of her sweet little friends BITE. Eeek!

We had to wait until after school when all the tiddlies had gone home. In the end the only people left were me, Ellie, Martha, Bianca and Ivy and Miss Pingle, but at least we'd had time to get Motley's box ready.

There was a great big bag of chicken food, and Martha loves food, so she took charge of putting it out.

If she'd been a chicken she'd have
eaten the whole lot at once, so she
wasn't too impressed when she was
only allowed to put a little bit on to a
tiny plastic saucer.

'That's not enough for thirteen
chickens!' said Martha. 'I'll go home
and get a cornflake bowl.'

'No!' said Miss Pingle.

Ivy filled up a little water bowl,
and me and Ellie put some kitchen
paper on the bottom of the box,

because that's what little chicks like to walk on.*

(* Interesting fact! Chickens don't like to walk on newspaper because it's too slippy for their feet, and they can get dirty from the ink too. And newspaper is covered in words but little chickens can't read so it's unfair on them. And that's true.)

Miss Pingle had got some wood

shavings to put in the box so the chickens could snuggle up and keep warm, and Bianca did a big sign with a picture of a chicken. Bianca does really good pictures, but I wanted her to draw a flower growing out of its bottom just like the one on the tiddlies picture! I was dying to ask her but then I thought she might get cross so I didn't.

Everything was ready when Mrs Twelvetrees came in carrying

46

the incubator. Inside were the little chickens.

HOORAY!

Mrs T went over to the window table and saw Bianca's sign.

'What a lovely picture,' said Mrs T. 'But isn't it supposed to have a flower growing out of its bottom?'

'HA HA HA' laughed Bianca.

Bah! I wish I'd asked now.

Mrs Twelvetrees checked inside the box.

'Well done chaps!' she said. 'I see you've put some kitchen paper down to stop them sliding about.'

'And to catch all the poo,' said Ivy.

'Er, yes,' said Mrs T. 'That too.'

Mrs T took the lid off the incubator. 'They've got quite warm in here, so let them have a little run around before you put them into Mr Motley's box.'

Mrs Twelvetrees put the incubator

on the floor and tipped it up a bit.
WEEE! The chickens all rolled out,
then they got on their feet and started
poddling around.

Awww . . . CUTE!

'The whole school is going to have
a big chicken assembly tomorrow
morning,' said Mrs T. 'So don't be
late, gang!' Then off she went to do
some other headteacher stuff.

The chickens were brilliant. There
was Wizzy who was really fast, and

Tubby who kept rolling over, and Bumper who kept climbing on top of Moody Broody who just sat there pulling cross faces.

I couldn't pick a favourite because they were all my favourite, but if I had to pick a *favourite* favourite, it would be Random. That's because the others kept bunching up together, but Random was far too busy. He toddled off to admire the new leaf on the rubber plant, then he inspected the radiator pipes and he finally ended up trying to peck a hole in Miss Pingle's bag.

It was all very jolly until a bad voice came from the doorway.

'What is going on in HERE?'

Oh potties. Miss Barking had come in. She's the deputy headteacher who has big square glasses and thinks that everything in the world is dangerous. One time she tried to shut the whole school because she saw a furry slug under the radiator in the library, but we all knew it was an old sweet. Of course we didn't tell her that, we just watched her freak out when Martha wiped the dust off and ate it HA HA wicked!

Standing behind her was Gwendoline Tutt.

'Look Miss Barking,' said Gwendoline with her horrible snotty voice. 'Those chickens are all over the floor. I don't think that's very hygienic, do you Miss Barking?'

Honestly! If anything isn't hygienic, it's Gwendoline. She always makes us feel sick. She must have been spying on us and then gone to fetch Miss Barking.

'Those chickens could be carrying a nasty disease,' said Miss Barking.

We were about to protest but then Random decided that Gwendoline's shoes were really interesting. He hurried over to have a good look.

Toddle toddle toddle – *poop!*

WAHOO WICKED! Random had done a little you-know-what right in front of Gwendoline! It was only the tiniest little blob that had splotted on to the floor but Gwendoline made the most of it.

'Urgh, that's totally GROSS!' she shouted then ran off out of the door.

What a baby! But Miss Barking wasn't taking any chances.

'Keep well back children,' said

Miss B staring at the blob like it was radioactive. 'There could be dangerous fumes filling the room.'

Huh.

She made us all line up against the far wall with the window open, then she reached into her bag and got out one of those paper face masks that go over your mouth and nose. When she put it on, her head looked like a giant potato wearing glasses.

'Do you have safety gloves Miss Pingle?' said the giant potato.

Miss Pingle shook her head.

'Really Miss Pingle,' said the

potato. 'Those little beaks are like needles and could inject you with chicken germs. Luckily for you, I have come prepared.'

Miss Barking pulled on a massive pair of gloves that made her hands look three times bigger. She got some wipes out of her bag to clear the little blob up, then she went crawling across the floor to catch the tiny little chickens. Poor things! Can you imagine being one day old and being chased by a giant potato with monster hands? Not nice.

Eventually she got all the chickens into Motley's box.

'We need to put the heater light on,' said Miss Pingle.

Miss Pingle was about to push the switch when Miss Barking stopped her.

'GLOVES!' said Miss B strictly. 'How do you know this electrical device is completely safe? Has it been tested? Does it have a certificate?'

Miss P sighed and let Miss Barking take over. Miss B clicked on the switch, but the light didn't come on.

'Just as I thought,' she said. 'It's broken.'

'Maybe you have to adjust the temperature with the knob,' suggested Miss P.

Miss Barking grabbed the knob in her big glove and turned it all the way up. The light came on.

'There,' she said.

'That looks a bit hot,' said Miss P. 'Can you turn it down a bit?'

Miss Barking grabbed the knob again and turned it back. The light went off.

'That's a bit too far,' said Miss Pingle.

'I KNOW what I'm doing thank you Miss Pingle!' said Miss Barking crossly, then she gave the knob one more turn.

'There . . . oh!'

Her giant hand had broken off the control knob! The light over the box was blazing full blast.

Yeep yeep yeep! went the chickens.

'Oh no!' said Ivy. 'Miss Barking is cooking the baby chickens!'

Miss Barking tried to push the knob back into place, but it kept falling off.

Eeek! I couldn't watch any more, so I ran off to get Motley. As soon as he came in and saw the light on full blast, he unplugged the box from the wall. Off it went –

phew!

Motley saw the broken knob lying on the table.

'Who did this?' he said crossly.

'I must go home,' said Miss Barking suddenly, and dashed out of the door still wearing her mask and gloves.

'Yes, fly back to your own planet,' muttered Motley as she went. He picked up the broken knob. 'It'll take me all night to fix it.'

'If the chickens don't have a heater, they'll get cold,' said Miss Pingle.

'We'll look after them,' I said. 'They can come and stay in our houses!'

Miss Pingle thought about it. 'As long as you keep them warm, they should be all right for one night,' she said. 'Just make sure they get plenty of water to drink.'

'And plenty of food,' said Martha

picking up the food bag.

Eeek! I suddenly had this vision of Martha shoving the whole bag inside one little chicken, and judging by Miss Pingle's face, she was having that same vision too!

'Put that down!' said Miss Pingle. 'That stays here.'

'So what can they eat?' demanded Martha.

'They can have Gilbert's food,' said Ivy. 'We've got loads of it.'

'Who's Gilbert?' asked Miss Pingle.

'Mum's goldfish,' said Ivy. 'But he's nearly dead so he doesn't need it.'

'NO!' said Miss Pingle firmly. 'The chickens will not need feeding for one night. But we do need something to keep them in.'

'There's a load of shoeboxes in Miss Bunn's class,' I said. 'We could use them to take the chickens home.'

'Not me!' whimpered Ellie. 'I

daren't! I had a bad dream about chickens.'

'Chickens aren't scary!' we said.

'They are when they've got poisonous beaks and peck through your tights,' said Ellie. 'My leg fell off.'

So I went to get four shoeboxes, one each for me, Martha, Ivy and Bianca, but not one for Ellie in case a chicken pecked through her tights and made her leg fall off.

'Thank you,' said Miss Pingle. 'I'll pack up the chickens and bring them down to the playground. You lot get your coats, and then ask your mums if you can take the chickens home.'

So we all whizzed out to the playground and asked our mums. Martha's mum got the wrong idea.

'You want to bring some chickens home?' said Martha's mum. 'But I've already got tea organised.

It's chops and veg.'

'We're not eating the chickens, Mum!' explained Martha. 'We're looking after them. Maybe we could give them some chops and veg for their tea.'

'NO!' we all said.

'They're right Martha,' said Martha's mum. 'I'm not going to let chickens eat your five-a-day.'

'Wow!' said Ivy. 'Do you get five vegetables Martha?'

'No,' said Martha. 'Five chops.'

Miss Pingle turned up with the four shoeboxes, and gave us one each apart from Ellie.

'I've taped down the lids, so don't open them until you get home,' said Miss P. 'And tonight, make sure they have a little bowl of water, and keep them warm. I want to see them all back tomorrow!'

Who's in the Box?

I made mum and Tilly walk home really fast because I couldn't wait to see who was in my box! As there were thirteen chickens, we should have got three chickens each, and then one lucky person would get an extra chicken. I was hoping I'd be the lucky one, and I

REALLY hoped the extra chicken was Random! Anybody who toddles up to Gwendoline and does a little poop right in front of her is my hero for life. He was so brill.

When we got in the front door, we saw lots of old towels on the stairs. Dad was halfway up trying to balance the stepladder on a kitchen chair. It looked lethal.

'Keep back!' said Dad. 'I'm decorating.'

72

'Have you got to do that now?' asked Mum.

'You're the one that wanted new wallpaper,' said Dad.

Mum couldn't be bothered to argue with him. She just told me to take the chickens upstairs out of the way.

I squeezed past the stepladder with Tilly following me. We went into our bedroom and I put the box on the chair. I was just about to open it . . .

BIG EXCITEMENT! . . .

but then Dad shouted:

'Agatha! Quick, I need you.'

I went out and saw he'd taken his shoes off and was balancing on the top banister rail. He was holding a tape measure up to the ceiling and I had to hold it at the bottom so he could see how high it was.

I was only gone for about five seconds, but if you've got a nosey interfering little sister, you'll know what's coming next.

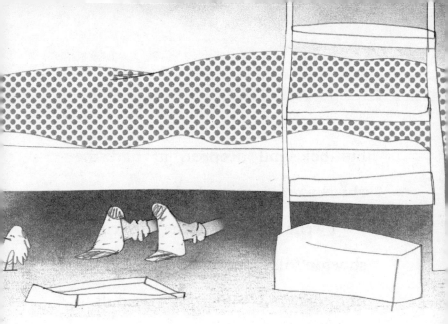

When I got back, the box was
upside down on the floor and Tilly's
legs were sticking out from under
our bunk beds. OOOOH I WAS SO
CROSS! Obviously she'd opened

75

the box and dropped it, and the chickens had run off to hide.

I crawled under the bunks and saw an old blue sock hopping up and down. I managed to grab it and found one of the chicks had got his head stuck inside the end. Tilly spotted another chicken right in the corner behind the leg of the bunk beds, pecking at a big hairy ball of fluff. I got them both out and put them back in the box, then I went back for another look.

There was no sign of any more, so we had to pull everything out. I found my horrible old woolly tartan tights which I'd stuffed down there years ago to lose them (yuk!). Plus there was my lost earphones (hooray!), pencils, old birthday cards, carrier bags, a gym shoe, some lego bricks, tons of hairy fluff, dead spiders, a not quite dead spider (EEEK!!!), and 17p in change.

'How many chickens were there in the box?' I asked Tilly.

'They ran off,' said Tilly.

That was a fat lot of use.

Just then there was a cross grumpy noise from outside the door.

'What's the matter, Dad?' I asked.

'I've just trod on something squishy.'

I dashed out to see him sitting on the carpet pulling his sock off. There was a yellow blob stuck on it.

'Oh no!' I said. 'It's one of our chickens!'

'A *chicken?*' said Dad.

He sniffed it.

'No, it's a bit of cake,' said Dad. 'What's a bit of cake doing up here? JAMES?'

At that point my brother James stuck his head out of his room.

'James, have you been bringing food upstairs?'

'Ummm,' said James shaking his

head, but it was obvious his mouth was full, plus he had crumbs all stuck to his jumper. In fact there was a trail of crumbs leading right along the landing, and there at the end was a little yellow thing happily helping himself.

'It's Tubby!' I said.

At last we had three chickens safely back in the box. One of them was definitely Tubby, but none of them was Random. Never mind.

Whoever they were, we were going to have a FAB time!

Chicken Football

· ·

After tea I thought my chickens needed some friends to play with, so I went next door to Martha's house.

I rang the bell but nothing happened. Maybe Martha was still having her tea? Then I had a nasty thought. I hope she wasn't trying to feed her chickens with chops and veg!

Suddenly there was a big POP sound from inside, then Martha opened the door.

'What was that noise?' I said.

'Just a balloon!' laughed Martha.

'Are you sure?' I said.

'Of course I'm sure,' said Martha. 'I was practising headers in the hall and it burst.'

'Thank goodness,' I said. 'I thought you'd been feeding your chickens with chops and veg and one of them had exploded.'

'Don't you trust me?' said Martha crossly, then she stomped off to get her shoebox. Inside were three little chickens.

'Happy now?' she said.

I felt a bit mean for upsetting Martha, but then I had the perfect idea to cheer her up again.

'How about if my chickens challenge your chickens to a

football match?'

'Wicked!' grinned Martha.

Martha brought her shoebox round to our house and we made a football pitch on the kitchen table with little lego goal posts. It was perfect because our table is up against the radiator so the chickens wouldn't get too cold. Martha put her chickens at one end, and I put mine at the other end, and we put an old ping pong ball in the middle.

It was really funny! The chickens toddled over and knocked the ball around. I suppose it should have been Martha's team against my team playing three-a-side, but it was more like one-a-side with six different sides.

If real football was like that with a ball as big as the people, it wouldn't be nearly so boring.

There was just one thing missing from the game. We hadn't got Random! Where was that star quality? Where was the creative play in midfield? Who was there to create chances and open up the defence? (No I don't know what any of that lot means either, but it's what they say on telly.) Actually Tubby did show a bit of star quality because he tried to eat one of the goal posts **ha ha!**

'We need more players,' said Martha.

'I'll get Ivy,' I said.

I left Martha and went to bang on Ivy's door, but then I looked up. Ivy was sitting by her bedroom window with her chickens running about on the windowsill.

'It's AGATHA!' shouted

Ivy to the chickens. 'Everybody wave at Agatha!'

Ivy held up one of her chickens and so I waved at it. Ivy waved back, but being mad she can't do a little wave. She did a giant big wave still holding the chicken.

'CAREFUL!' I shouted.

Ivy disappeared from the window then I heard her come downstairs, four at a time (as usual).

WAM BAM BAM WUMP!

Ivy's door opened and there she was with her shoe box.

'We're having a chicken football match,' I said.

'Awesome!' said Ivy.

'How many have you got?'

'Three,' said Ivy.

'Are you sure?' I asked her. 'What about the one you were waving?'

'You mean Mr Thompson?' asked Ivy. 'He's back in the box.'

'Can I see?' I said. I felt I had to

90

check. It's not that I don't trust Ivy, it's just that Ivy is mad.

Ivy opened her box. Sure enough she had three chickens.

'There's Mr Thompson,' she said. 'And that's Lovely, and that's Drain Pump.'

Ha ha! I didn't expect Ivy to give her chickens normal names, but where did she get Drain Pump from?

'It's in the book I'm reading,' said Ivy.

'What book?'

'Washing machine instructions,' said Ivy. 'I've only got four more pages to go.'

You see what I mean about Ivy? Mad mad mad.

Soon we had nine chickens running around on the kitchen table. It wasn't hard to tell who they all were. I had Tubby and my other two were Bib and Bob. Martha had brought Wizzy and Bumper and one with an extra little funny tuft of fluff she called Peckham. Ivy's chickens were all huddled together like a ball with six legs, but there was still no sign of Random.

'Bianca must have the other four chickens,' I said. 'Let's see if she wants to bring hers round too.'

So Martha went to Bianca's house and came back with her shoebox.

'Is Bianca coming?' I said.

'No, she's got to do her trombone

practice,' said Martha. 'But she said we can borrow her chickens.'

We opened up Bianca's box . . . *OH DEAR!*

We had expected to see four chickens, but there were only three. Straight away, I knew which one was missing!

Where was Random?

I was worried sick. When Tilly had let the chickens escape from my box, I thought I'd caught them all.

Maybe I hadn't? Maybe Random was still running around somewhere?

I had to try and keep cool so that Martha and Ivy didn't know what I was thinking. I decided to double-check their stories.

'So Martha,' I said. 'Are you sure you didn't feed your chickens any chops and veg? Not even one little chop and a tiny bit of cabbage?'

'And one drop of gravy?' asked Ivy.

95

'Why?' asked Martha.

'I just thought that maybe one of your chickens exploded and you'd forgotten?'

'NO WAY!' snapped Martha.

It was getting a bit nasty so I quickly turned to Ivy.

'So Ivy,' I said. 'You've got three chickens now, but think carefully. When you opened the box, was it a different number?'

'Like what?' said Ivy.

'Like *four* perhaps?' I said. 'It's just that I saw you waving Mr Thompson around . . .'

'And you're saying I might have accidentally thrown a chicken away are you?' said Ivy.

'I didn't say that . . .'

'But you MEANT it.'

It was getting nasty again, but I was saved by the front door bell ringing. It was Ivy's mum and she was looking very sad.

'Can Ivy come home?' she asked. 'Just for a minute?'

'What for?' said Ivy.

'I need you,' said Ivy's mum. Then she started to sniff and wipe her eyes, so Ivy went to see what the matter was.

What's Tocking the Bloob Up?

After Ivy had gone, me and Martha put the chickens back into their boxes. It was awful, because we were both counting them over and over, but it didn't make any difference. There were only twelve when it should have been thirteen.

'It wasn't me that lost a chicken,' said Martha. 'Maybe it was you?'

'No no, not me, impossible,' I said. I was trying to act casual but my voice went all squeaky and I know I was going red.

Then Dad came into the kitchen to get a bucket of water.

'Be careful on the stairs Agatha,' said Dad. 'It's all a bit sticky, so don't let those chickens go running round up there again. Remember, I nearly

100

trod on one.'

Off he went. Martha was staring at me furiously.

'You were trying to blame me and Ivy!' she snapped. 'And all the time I bet it's your fault.'

'No no no!' I said. 'Maybe Bianca knows what's happened. Let's go and ask her.'

'We can't ask her now,' said Martha. 'She's playing her trombone. Listen, you'll hear it.'

101

So we listened, but the funny thing was that we *didn't* hear it!

Normally when Bianca plays her trombone everybody on Odd Street can hear her going *bwarb bab barp*. One time she was learning a new note called BOTTOM B FLAT which made all the glasses rattle in our cupboard ha ha! My brother James does a few BOTTOM B FLAT noises sometimes, and he doesn't even have a trombone. Typical boy.

Martha and me went outside, but we still couldn't hear anything even though Bianca's bedroom window was open. We saw her moving about inside.

'Hey Bianca!' shouted Martha. 'We thought you were playing your trombone.'

'I'm trying,' said Bianca. 'But something is tocking the bloob up.'

Tocking the bloob up? We love Bianca, but sometimes she takes a bit

103

of working out. She had another go.

'It's bloobing the tock up.'

It was no good, so instead of trying to explain any more, Bianca stuck her trombone out the window and gave it a mighty blow. Her face went bright red and her cheeks stuck out like she was swallowing two apples at once, but no sound came out.

'I know what she means!' I said.

'Me too!' said Martha.

'Something is *blocking the tube up*!' we both said.

We were having a good laugh when suddenly . . .

PLOP . . . BWARBBBB . . . weeeee!

A fluffy yellow lump shot out of the end of the trombone along with a massive blast of BOTTOM B FLAT. It flew over our heads and normally Odd Street is really empty because cars can't go past the end, but just then Gwendoline Tutt went by on her pink bike and it landed on her shoulder.

'Did you see that?' gasped Martha.

'It was Random!' I said. 'He must have got out of Bianca's box and climbed into her trombone.'

By this time Gwendoline was up
the street past number 13, and me
and Martha were running after her.

'Gwendoline!' we
shouted. 'COME BACK!'

'Can't catch me, losers!'
said Gwendoline, and she
pedalled faster.

Gwendoline's house is
number 59, and we had
to run all the way there
before she stopped. We

were puffed out.

'What do you two want?' demanded Gwendoline.

'Don't move,' I said. 'There's something on your shoulder. Let me get it.'

But just as I was reaching out, Gwendoline noticed the yellow thing. She screamed and brushed it off on to the ground.

'UGH! What is it?' she shouted.

'It's a chicken,' we said.

'It looks dead,' said Gwendoline. 'Serves it right.'

OOOOOH, I WAS SO CROSS! (Even crosser than I was with Tilly on page 75.)

When Gwendoline opened their garage door to put her bike away, I could see all her dad's gardening stuff. Suddenly the lawnmower started itself and ate Gwendoline up then did a big burp YIPPEE! Actually it didn't but I promise you, if I was making this story up then I would have put that bit in for definite.

Meanwhile Martha had bent down to look at the yellow thing.

'I don't think it's the right colour,' said Martha.

She picked it up, just using her fingertips. Martha was right. I didn't know what it was, but at least I knew what it wasn't. It wasn't Random thank goodness!

It was like a yellow fluffy sausage

with a bit of string tied to the end. We took it back down the street and held it up so Bianca could see it.

'That's my trombone cleaner!' said Bianca. 'I was looking for that.'

'Gwendoline just tried to kill it,' said Martha.

'She's nuts,' said Bianca.

Oh well. At least Random hadn't been blasted across the road by a BOTTOM B FLAT, but where was he?

A Sad Goodbye

When me and Martha got back into my house, Ellie came round to see the chickens. Typical Ellie, she loves numbers so the first thing she did was count them.

'There's only twelve!' said Ellie.

'We know,' I said. 'It's really freaking us out.'

112

'I'll tell you something even freakier,' said Ellie. 'Ivy was in her yard talking to a cactus in a plant pot.'

'WHAT???'

Ivy lives next door at number 7, and the only place you can see her yard from is our bathroom window so we all headed for the stairs.

Dad was on top of his wobbly ladder holding a long bit of soggy wallpaper.

'Where are you lot going?'

he said.

'To the bathroom,' I said.

'All of you?' said Dad.

'Can't it wait?'

'No!' we said and squeezed ourselves past the ladder.

'CAREFUL!' said Dad, then he fell against the wall and got the paper stuck to his trousers which was dead funny but we didn't stop to laugh. We had stuff to do.

Our bathroom window has fuzzy glass fixed in at the bottom, so the only way you can see out is if you balance on the edge of the bath and open the window at the top. *Warning:*

make sure the toilet lid is down. One time Dad left the lid up when he climbed on the bath to change the lightbulb, then he slipped and his foot ended up in the toilet water ha ha!

So there we all were on the edge of the bath looking down into Ivy's back yard. All we could see was a little cactus in a pot sitting on a kitchen chair looking very important.

'See?' said Ellie. 'I told you it was freaky.'

Yes, it was a bit freaky, but it was nothing compared to some of the other things in Ivy's yard. For instance it looks like there's a row of sticks growing out of the window box, but actually it's all the arms and legs that Ivy pulled off her Barbies.

We were still staring at the cactus when Ivy came out of her back door. She was wearing a black top hat from her dressing up box and she was carrying a piece of paper with writing on. She walked round and round the little cactus very slowly making low bell noises like this:

Dung . . . dung . . . dung . . .

Then she stood in front of the cactus and held up the paper to read it. This is what she said:

Go to sleep my funny friend,

Rest your little head

Your lovely dreams won't stop

because you won't wake up.

You're dead.

It's sad we have to say goodbye,

And I don't want to spoil it.

That's why you're buried in a pot

And not flushed down the toilet.

Then Ivy bent down, gave the cactus pot a little kiss, and went back indoors.

We all went very quiet.

Then all at once we went **EEEK!**

☆ The Magic Cactus

· ·

Me and Ellie and Martha were back in our kitchen feeling a bit freaked out.

'Do you think Ivy had the extra chicken and buried it in the cactus pot?' said Ellie.

'She told us she only had three,' I said. 'And Ivy doesn't lie.'

It's true, she doesn't. Ivy might pull her dolls apart and she might run up the going-down escalator at the shopping centre and she might pull her tights on over her head to pretend she's got legs growing out of her ears, but Ivy does not lie.

But we had to be sure, and we couldn't exactly ask her could we? We couldn't say, 'Did you kill Random and bury him in a plant pot?'

'There's only one thing for it,' I

said. 'We'll have to sneak into Ivy's yard and empty the pot out.'

'Ivy will know we've been in,' said Martha. 'My mum sells those cactuses in her shop and if you tip one out it goes all over the place.'

'That's right,' said Ellie. 'We got one last year, just like Ivy's. Same pot and everything.'

Suddenly I was pulling at my hair. It's what I always do when I'm getting a brilliant idea.

'Have you still got that cactus?'
I asked.

'Of course,' said Ellie.

'Bingo!'

Before we get any further, I have
to tell you that the old man who
types these books out for me has been
having a little moan. He said there's
no such word as *cactuses*. When you
have more than one cactus, they
should be called *cacti*. That's because
cactus is a Latin word which is how

the ancient Romans used to talk, and if Julius Caesar was giving a bunch of them to his mum, he would have called it a bunch of *cacti*. But Julius Caesar and that lot all popped their clogs about 2,000 years ago, so how does the old man know this eh? I know he's a bit doddery, but 2,000 years old? Anyway, I made him test it out on the internet, and it turns out you're allowed to say cactuses OR cacti, so if anybody asks you, now you know. And he has to stop moaning.

Right then, where had we got to? Oh yes, I know. Ellie said she had a cactus like Ivy's and that gave me a really good idea so I said 'bingo'. **WAHOO!** On we go then . . .

There's a back alley that runs behind the houses in Odd Street. Everybody has a gate from the alley into their yard so you can put dustbins out and put your bike away

and so on. Ivy's gate is never locked
because strangers wouldn't dare go
in. As soon as they saw the freaky
bits of doll sticking out of the window
box, they'd turn round and run a
mile ha ha!

I explained my plan.

'Ellie, all you have to do is take your cactus out of your back gate, sneak into Ivy's yard and swap them over. Then we can take Ivy's cactus somewhere safe and have a look inside it.'

'Me?' gasped Ellie. 'But what if Ivy or her mum see me? They might think I'm a burglar and I might go to prison, then I'd miss school and Mrs Twelvetrees would send my mum a note and if mum got a note she'd be really upset!'

Poor Ellie. She's not really the best person to send on dangerous missions because she's so scared of everything.

'You'll be fine,' I assured her. 'Me and Martha will make sure they're both at the front door, so they won't see you.'

'Promise?'

'Absolutely promise,' I said.

I got our spare door key out of the kitchen drawer and showed it to the others.

'This is all we need,' I said. 'Come on!'

★

A few minutes later, I was by Ivy's front door, and Martha was outside Ellie's house which is the next one along. I put the key on the pavement then I rang Ivy's bell. When she opened the door she still had her black top hat on.

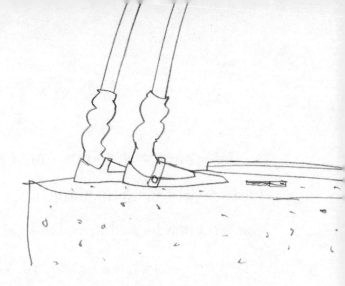

'*Dung dung dung*,' said Ivy making

the bell noise. 'I'm very busy! *Dung.*'

'But it's important,' I said and I

pointed at the key. 'Is that yours?'

Ivy came out to have a look. 'I

don't know,' she said.

'Only one way to find out,' I said
and I pulled the door shut.

'You just locked me out!' said Ivy
crossly.

'It's so we can test the key,' I said.

So we tested it and it didn't work.
(Surprise surprise!)

'Sorry,' I said. 'Never mind. You
better ring the bell and get your
mum to open the door.'

Ivy reached for the bell and I
winked at Martha, then Martha

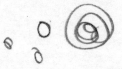

gave a thumbs up through Ellie's
window. Ellie was waiting inside and
it was the signal for her to get going!
By the time Ivy's mum had come to
let Ivy back in, Ellie would have done
the swap. Easy.

But then Ivy didn't ring the bell.

'I just remembered, Mum's
getting in the bath,' said Ivy.

Oh no! Ivy's bathroom window
looked out over the yard just like ours
did. If Ivy's mum happened to look

out at the wrong time . . . eeek!
Panic panic.

'Quick!' I said. 'Ring the bell
before she gets in.'

'I better not,' said Ivy. 'I'll just
go round to the alley and get in the
back way.'

'NO!' I said. 'No, you can't! Just
ring the bell.'

'Don't worry,' said Ivy about to
run off. 'It'll only take me a second.'

What could I do? Ellie was

already on her way, we had to save her!

Luckily Martha had the answer. She just walked up to Ivy's front door and pushed the bell and kept her finger on it.

BURRRINGGGGGGGGGGG!

'Stop it stop it!' said Ivy. 'Mum'll go nuts!'

Ivy tried to pull Martha off, but Martha is too big and strong.

'Sorry Ivy,' said Martha. 'It's

Agatha's idea.'

Well, that wasn't very nice was it?

Ivy just stood there hating me while Martha kept her finger on the bell. Eventually we heard some muttering and moaning from inside.

'Time to go,' said Martha, and then quick as a flash she dashed away. Gosh it's amazing how fast she can move for a big person.

The door opened and Ivy's mum was there wrapped in a big towel looking very cross with bubbles all over her toes.

'Ivy Malting, you're the devil's own child. Why do you go dragging your poor mother out of the bath?'

'Agatha locked me out!' said Ivy.

'I've a good mind to lock you out myself,' said Ivy's mum. 'Now come in and take that hat off. It's giving me the creeps.'

The doorbell thing was all a bit embarrassing, but soon Martha and

Ellie and me had met up in our yard
with Ivy's cactus. I thought cactuses
were supposed to be green, but this
one was more like grey and it looked
a bit dead. When we tipped it out,
there was a little lumpy white paper
bag rolled up in the bottom.

'It looks very small,' said Ellie.

'Random was only a baby,' I
said and we were all nearly crying.

'Do you think chickens have
ghosts?' asked Ellie which made us

laugh as well as crying at the same time. It was bit like boo hoo HA HA boo hoo HA HA and it gives you a really runny nose.

Martha picked the bag up with the very ends of her fingertips in case she got ghost chicken germs. It didn't look quite right. To start with, the bag was soaking wet and the lump we could see through the paper was more orange than yellow. Martha unrolled it and we looked inside.

It was a fish!

'That's Gilbert,' said Ellie. 'Ivy said he was poorly, and now he's dead.'

No wonder Ivy's mum had been so upset when she came round to our house. She'd had Gilbert for years, she used to teach him tricks and everything.

Suddenly a loud shriek came over the wall from Ivy's yard.

'WOW oh WOW oh WOW!' we heard Ivy screaming. 'WOWWWW!'

We charged in the back door and up the stairs past Dad on the wobbly ladder . . .

'**DO YOU MIND???**' shouted Dad.

'Sorry Dad!'

. . . and then into the bathroom, climbed on the bath and looked out of the window.

Ivy was staring at the cactus.

'She's noticed it's different,' said Martha.

'But I thought they were exactly the same,' I said.

'They used to be,' said Ellie. 'But there was something I forgot to tell you . . .'

But before Ellie could finish, Ivy picked up the cactus and turned it round.

'Wow!' said me and Martha.

'That's what I forgot to tell you,' said Ellie. 'Our cactus grew a pink flower.'

'Hey Mum!' shouted Ivy running into her house. 'Our cactus is MAGIC!'

We were so busy giggling that our feet slipped off the bath, and guess what? We'd forgotten to shut the toilet lid so Martha ended up with her foot in the toilet ha ha!

The Lump of Doom

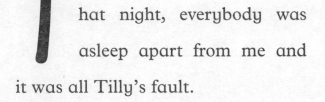

That night, everybody was asleep apart from me and it was all Tilly's fault.

If she hadn't opened the shoebox and let the chickens out, then I'd have known for sure if there had been three or four. As it was, I was lying awake on the top bunk worring myself silly about Random, while she was nicely asleep on the bottom bunk doing funny little *moo* sounds into her pillow. Evil child.

The shoebox was on the chair with the three chickens snuggled up inside making little chicken snorey noises. All I could do was lie there and listen out for anything that might have been Random walking around the house.

It was exactly 02:31 on my alarm clock when I heard a very quiet little tapping noise. It was coming from out on the landing.

I whizzed out and clicked the light on. The sound stopped, and there was nothing moving. Dad had been really late finishing the wallpaper, and the towels were still all over the place. I went down the stairs, picking them up and having a look, but there was no sign of Random. When I got

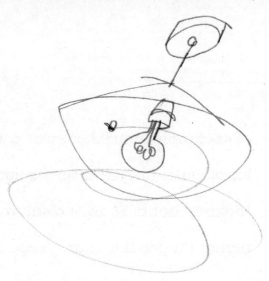

to the bottom I heard the tapping again. It was a bug flying round in the light shade. Boring!

I set off back up the stairs. Mum wasn't going to be too happy with the wallpaper! It was all wonky with lots

149

of sticky bits, and there was a weird lump under the paper by the top step. It was about the size of a sausage, or perhaps a potato . . . or an egg . . . or a *baby chicken!*

PANIC PANIC!

It was obvious what must have happened. When Dad was waving his wet paper around, Random had got stuck to it and now he was glued to the wall!

I stared at the lump to see if it

was moving. It wasn't. I put my ear to it and listened. No sound.

'Random, are you in there?' I whispered.

The lump didn't answer. Then I remembered how Miss Bunn got the chickens to talk. I clicked my tongue a bit then started to sing:

Chick chick chick chick CHICKEN!
Lay a little egg for me.

Chick chick chick chick

CHICKEN!

I want one for my tea.

As I was singing, I started picking at the edge of the wallpaper to see if I could peel it back.

'What are you doing?' said James.

Oh potties! I looked up and saw James watching me over the banister.

'I was just getting a drink of water,' I said and stood up.

'Liar,' said James. 'Your singing woke me up. And why are you trying to pull the wallpaper off?'

'Don't be silly,' I said. 'You're having a dream.'

All I could do was get back into bed and hope that James would forget all about it.

I plomped my head on the pillow and shut my eyes but then I heard a scratching sound outside the door. I wasn't going to get up in case James was still around, but the scratching got bigger and bigger. Suddenly there was a massive rip of paper and then I heard creaky footsteps coming into the bedroom.

'Ag – ath – aaar!' said a screechy voice. 'Agathaaar, why didn't you save meee?'

'Who are you?' I said, only I didn't say it because when I talked I could only make chicken noises. *Eeeep peep zik!*

'I am Ran-DOOOOM, the chicken ghost! Why didn't you save meee?'

EEEKY FREAK! I rolled up into a tiny ball under my duvet.

'It wasn't my fault!' I said but it came out like *deek eeep wee!*

I knew something very big was looking over the edge of the top bunk.

'Answer me or I will peck through your tights.'

Eh? I wasn't wearing tights. I was in bed. But then I felt my legs. Oh no, I WAS wearing tights! It was my horrible old woolly tartan tights too. How did they get there?

'I will peck through your tights and your LEG WILL FALL OFF . . . leg will fall off . . . leg will fall off . . .'

And then I woke up.

Bah! I felt like such a clot. I'd been having Ellie's dream about chickens. I sat up and pulled my hair to get my brain working. There was no giant chicken, I wasn't wearing tights, and it was the morning because I could hear voices out on the landing.

'It looks awful,' said Mum. 'We'll have to save up to get a proper decorator in.'

'If that's what you want,' said

Dad. 'Or we could leave it and save up for concert tickets instead?'

'Woo-hoo good idea!' cheered Mum. 'But we must get rid of that big lump.'

A big lump? So the lump wasn't part of the dream. Maybe Random was in there after all?

By the time I was dressed, the others were down in the kitchen still having the wallpaper conversation.

'You could try squashing that

lump down with your foot,' said
Mum.

'NO!' I said a bit too loudly.

'Agatha's right,' said Dad. 'It
might make a nasty mess.'

EEEK! If that lump was what
I thought it was, then it would be a
lot nastier than Dad was expecting!

'What do you think the lump is?'
asked Mum.

I'm glad she was asking Dad
and not me.

'A big blob of wet glue,' said Dad. 'I could stick a pin in, then squeeze it so it all comes out.'

'NO NO YOU CAN'T!' I screamed.

'Are you alright?' Dad asked.

'Ignore her,' said James who was in there eating his cornflakes. 'She was singing about chickens to that lump last night. She's gone bonkers.'

'I have NOT gone bonkers,' I said.

And that's when Dad looked out of the kitchen door and said: 'Speaking of chickens, there's a giant chicken coming down the stairs.'

ARGHHH!

I was about to dive under the table, when I suddenly realised . . .

'This is another dream, isn't it?' I said. 'I'm not awake at all. There's no giant chicken.'

'Yes there is,' said Dad.

'He's right, there is,' said Mum

162

who had gone to look.

'No there ISN'T!' I said crossly. 'I *know* it's a dream. None of this is real!'

And just to show it was a dream and nothing really mattered and we'd all wake up, I got on the table, picked up the cornflake box and tipped it out all over my head.

'See?' I said. 'I wouldn't be doing this if it was real, would I?'

Mum and Dad looked at me

like I was an alien. Then Tilly came in through the door wearing her chicken head and some yellow tights and a yellow T-shirt and a set of fairy wings.

'What's Agatha doing?' asked Tilly.

'Agatha thought you were a real chicken,' laughed James.

'Tilly's dressed up for the school chicken assembly,' explained Mum. 'It's a very good costume Tilly!'

'It certainly fooled Agatha,' said Dad.

Don't Count Your Chickens Before They Hatch!

On the way to school, I met up with the others. We had four shoeboxes with three chickens each.

'Three times four makes twelve,' said Ellie who's our numbers expert.

'Can't it make thirteen sometimes?' asked Martha hopefully.

'Never!' said Ellie strictly. 'So
there's nothing you can do about it.'

It was all right for Ellie. She was
the only one of us who KNEW she
hadn't lost a chicken. The rest of us
were worried sick.

Motley was waiting for us by
the school entrance.

'Mrs Twelvetrees wants me to
put the chickens in the brooding

box ready for the assembly,' he said holding his hands out.

All we could do was pass the boxes over and hope that nobody else remembered how many chickens there were supposed to be.

By the time we'd put our coats and bags away, we were the last people into the hall. There was a great big sheet of cardboard in the middle of the floor and all the tiddlies were sitting round it wearing their chicken hats and any other dressing up clothes they had. The place was full of cowboy chickens, fairy chickens, alien chickens and one little tiddly tot had put on his Halloween outfit and come as a chicken-headed pumpkin. EEEEK!

Everybody else had to stand round behind the tiddlies. Me and Martha and Ivy and Bianca stayed close to the door in case we needed to make a quick escape. If the tiddlies realised there was a chicken missing, it would be nasty. None of us wanted to face up to an angry chicken-headed pumpkin.

Mrs Twelvetrees was standing next to Motley's brooding box and right beside her was Miss Barking looking very serious. Miss B had her mask and big gloves on, and she was holding a little fishing net on the end of a stick. **Thank goodness!** We could all relax knowing that if a chicken decided to go mental and attack our beloved headteacher, then Miss Barking would dive in and save her. YAY! Give that woman a medal.

Mrs Twelvetrees clapped her hands and we all went quiet.

recycle

'What a thrilling day!' gushed Mrs Twelvetrees. 'We're here to welcome our new visitors, the chickens!'

'HOORAY!' cheered everybody.

'Miss Bunn's class gave all the chickens special names,' said Mrs T. 'Who can remember their names?'

Over by the door we breathed a big sigh of relief *PHEW!* There was no way the tiddlies would remember thirteen different names, so nobody would realise there was one missing.

Flozzie Slippin put her hand up. 'I can remember the names,' she said.

'What are they?' asked Mrs Twelvetrees.

'One, Two, Three, Four, Five, Six, Seven, Eight, Nine, Ten, Eleven, Twelve and Thirteen!'

'That's right Flozzie,' said Mrs T. 'The chickens are named after the numbers!'

Oh no! That was NOT what we wanted to hear.

'So how many chickens should we have in here?' asked Mrs Twelvetrees tapping the brooding box. She was really rubbing it in.

'Thirteen!' cheered all the tiddlies.

'And who can count to thirteen?' asked Mrs T.

'We can!' cheered the tiddlies.

We all felt really awful, and then Mrs T made it even worse.

'Before we count the chickens, let's have a big clap for our chicken monitors who looked after them last night. Well done Ivy, Martha, Agatha and Bianca. Where are you chaps?'

Mrs Twelvetrees was peering round the hall. We sneaked towards the door, but Miss Pingle had got in the way.

'Here they are!' called out Miss Pingle helpfully.

'**HURRAH!**' cheered all the tiddlies and everybody gave us a big clap.

Normally I like getting a big clap, but all I could think about was the lump in the wallpaper. If anybody ever found out about it then I'd have to hide in a dustbin and grow a beard.

'Let's have the first chicken, Miss Barking,' said Mrs Twelvetrees.

'Everybody get ready to count!'

Miss Barking went up to the box and reached in, but then she stopped and pulled a puzzled face.

'She's noticed!' gasped Martha. 'Stand by for big trouble.'

'Come along Miss Barking,' said Mrs Twelvetrees. 'The gang's all waiting!'

Miss Barking got a chicken out and carefully put it on the cardboard.

'One!' counted the tiddlies.

'He's lovely!' gushed Mrs Twelvetrees.

'That's not Lovely, that's Drain Pump,' whispered Ivy.

Miss Barking kept going.

'Two, three, four . . .' counted the tiddlies as the chickens arrived and huddled together on the cardboard.

'Five, six, seven, eight, nine . . .'

'Isn't this FUN?' said Mrs T.

'Ten, eleven . . .' chanted the tiddlies.

But then Miss Barking stopped. She was staring in the box again.

'Come along Miss Barking,' said Mrs T. 'We want to see all the thirteen chickens then put them back before they get cold.'

'Oh dear,' said Miss Barking and then she pulled out the twelfth chicken.

'Twelve!' cheered the tiddlies.

Everybody sat waiting for the thirteenth chicken.

Miss Barking obviously didn't know what to do. She was still staring into the box.

'Something has gone wrong,' said Miss Barking.

'Oh!' said all the tiddlies. Everybody was sounding really worried.

'They are so going to hate us,' I said.

'I don't blame them,' said Martha sadly. 'I hate us too.'

Miss Barking started fiddling with the red light over Motley's box and prodded the control.

'I said it wasn't safe,' she said. 'But they never listen.'

Mrs Twelvetrees went to have a look.

'What is it?' she said, then looked into the box. 'GOOD GOLLY!'

Very carefully she reached her hands in and pulled out . . . a purple chicken!

'THIRTEEN!' shouted the tiddlies.

'*Thirteen?*' we gasped.

Mrs T put the purple chicken on the floor, and it wasn't any old purple chicken either! He toddled straight over to where Gwendoline was standing and did a great big POOP!

WAHOO!

There was only one little fluffy person it could be . . . RANDOM!

Who Did It
and How?

● ●

The rest of Friday was a complete blur. We must have had lessons and lunchtime and playtime and everything, but I couldn't concentrate. All I could think about was the big mystery. How did Random get to be purple?

The last lesson was a number test and Miss Pingle handed out quiz sheets for us to fill in. Everybody else started writing, but I was too busy looking round the class for clues. Some purple chicken footprints next to a big pot of purple paint would have been helpful, but I couldn't see any of that. All I could see was Liam quietly slipping an old apple core into Matty's reading bag ha ha! Actually you shouldn't laugh at boys it only encourages them.

I started to doodle on the corner of the sheet. **Big mistake!** The next thing I knew, everybody was getting ready to go home and Ivy was shaking my shoulder.

'Come on Agatha!' she said. 'Haven't you finished?'

I looked down at my sheet. I'd done a brilliant chicken with thirty wings and beaks and teeth and a flower growing out of its bottom.

'Very nice!' laughed Ivy. 'But you better get some answers in quick. We'll wait for you out by the gates.'

Soon there was just me and Miss Pingle left in the classroom. I was madly trying to fill the sheet in while she was packing her bag up.

'Time to go Agatha!' she said. 'It's the weekend. I've got plans, and I'm afraid they don't include you.'

She came to take the sheet off me, but as soon as she walked away

from the bag, it fell
over. Everything slid
out on to the floor.
'Oh no!' she
said. 'It always
does that.'

She stood the bag up but before she could put anything back in, it fell over again.

'Why don't you get another bag?' I asked.

'I should do,' she admitted. 'But I just love the colour too much.'

The colour?

I found myself staring at the bag and then at Miss Pingle's hair. I was getting a mad idea, and I expect I was pulling a mad face to go with it.

'Agatha?' said Miss Pingle. 'Hello? Are you all right?'

'Fine!' I said. 'I just wanted to ask you something. Did you notice anything unusual about the thirteenth chicken today?'

'Er . . . why?' asked Miss Pingle. She sounded a bit nervous, and she had every reason to be!

'What colour would you say that chicken was?'

'A sort of purple,' said Miss P.

'Oh really?' I said. 'Because if you ask me, I'd say it was more like . . . *Damson Dream!*'

Miss Pingle stared down at her bag, and gave her hair a stroke at the same time.

'Did you dye him to match your hair?' I asked.

'NO!' exclaimed Miss P.

She tried not to look at me but I was giving her a HARD STARE. It was like slowly squishing a banana.

There was nothing Miss Pingle could do to resist my awesome eyeball power!

'Well, I didn't do it on purpose,' she said. 'Honest!'

'Let me guess,' I said. 'When the chickens were running round yesterday, your bag fell over and he sneaked in.'

'He must have done,' said Miss Pingle. 'Then when I got home, my bag fell over again. He hopped out and ran to hide behind my bin.'

'And he found some of your hair dye.'

Miss Pingle nodded.

'There was a tissue on the floor with a big blob on it, and he got tangled up in it. I tried to wash the dye off with a bit of warm water, but he turned purple!'

Poor Miss P. The only thing she could do after that was sneak him back into school and slip him into the brooding box before the assembly.

'I'm just glad that none of you spent last night worrying about where he was,' said Miss P.

'Oh no, of course not,' I said.

Well I was hardly going to admit I thought Random was a giant chicken ghost that had come out of a lump in our wallpaper and made me tip cornflakes all over my head, was I?

The Odd Street Miracle

....

That's the end of the main story, but there is one more thing to tell you, because it's my favourite part! It's even better than when Martha's foot went in the toilet. Well, it is for me anyway.

It happened just after I'd seen Miss

195

Pingle. I met all the others out in the playground and we had a slow wander up Odd Street back to our houses. They had a good laugh when I told them what had happened to Random.

'Will he be purple forever?' asked Ellie.

'Only until his guff flows,' said Bianca.

'Until his *guff flows*?' said everybody.

'His guff flows and then he fets

his gethers,' said Bianca.

It took me a minute before I got it.

'His *fluff goes*, and then he *gets* his *feathers*!' I said.

By the time we'd worked out what Bianca was saying, we were standing outside number 1 where she lives.

'Bye bye Bianca,' I said. 'Sorry I blamed you for blowing a chicken out of your trombone!'

'That's OK,' said Bianca. In she went.

Next it's Martha's house at number 3.

'Sorry I blamed you for making Random explode,' I said.

'That's OK,' said Martha and she went in too.

When we got to number 5 where I live, there was just Ivy and Ellie left.

'I'm *really* sorry about your cactus, Ivy,' I said.

'Our cactus?' asked Ivy. 'What's our cactus got to do with you?'

Oops!

I shouldn't have said anything, because Ellie got into a real panic.

'Nothing's the matter,' said Ellie. 'Nothing. **NOTHING.**'

Ellie ran off into her house at number 9.

Ivy gave me a suspicious look.

'What's been going on?' she asked.

But before I could think of what to say, Ivy's front door opened.

'Bless you, Mary!' said a big booming voice from inside. 'I'm so glad you asked me round.'

'That sounds like Father Bartles,' said Ivy. 'He's the priest from our church.'

A very big man in black clothes

stepped out followed by Ivy's mum. He scratched his chin thoughtfully.

'Are you *sure* that cactus was dead yesterday morning?' he asked.

'Dead as a nail,' said Ivy's mum. 'And so that little flower must be a present from my dear Gilbert up in heaven! I'm right, aren't I Father?'

'Why not?' laughed Father Bartles. 'I'll write it up in my parish report. I shall call it the Odd Street Miracle!'

Ivy's mum did a little happy hoppy skip, just like Ivy does, and she had the BIGGEST smile on her face.

Father Bartles got on his bike and then, with a bit of a wobble, pedalled off down the road. 'See you on Sunday!' he shouted.

Ivy's mum kept waving after him, even when he'd disappeared round the corner. Then she did another little happy hoppy skip and went inside.

Ivy grabbed me and gave me a big hug.

'Thanks for cheering her up,' she said.

'Me?' I said. 'What did I do?'

'I don't know,' admitted Ivy. 'But the cactus, the flower, Mum being happy again . . . it HAS to be something to do with you!'

I was just about to tell her, but she covered up her ears.

'Oh no, don't tell me!' said Ivy.

'Then it wouldn't be a miracle any more!'

Then she ran inside shouting 'MIRACLE MIRACLE MIRACLE!' and slammed her door with a great big WHAM.

So that's official then. It was a miracle and everybody on Odd Street lived happily ever after!

Even the cactus had a good time because Ivy kept putting little bits of fish food in the plant pot in case

Gilbert's ghost was feeling hungry. And that's not a joke because we all believe in ghosts in Odd Street because our school had one!

I'm not kidding. It was a horrible figure that glowed in the dark and we ALL saw it through the windows **EEEKY FREAK!** It all started when . . . oh sorry!

I'll have to tell you about the ghost another time because the old man who's typing this book out says we've only got a few pages left and I've got a puzzle for you to try! I wasn't going to tell you the answer, but the old man said that was unfair, so here's a little secret – the answer is on page 106, 7 lines down and it's the last word but DON'T LOOK YET!

Before you put this book away, if you've read it all by yourself then you deserve a big treat. Bend your mouth round and give yourself a big

KISS on the cheek. **Ha ha** don't worry! I'm only kidding so don't bother – unless you want to of course.

See you next time and good luck with the puzzle!

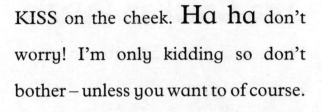

BYEEEEEEEE . . .

The End

The Chicken Puzzle

by Agatha Jane Parrot

There were four eggs in Miss Bunn's class painted blue, pink, green and yellow. Four chickens, called Wizzy, Tubby, Drain Pump and Random, hatched out of the eggs. Here are some clues:

- The green egg was the second to hatch.

- Drain Pump was the third chicken to hatch but he did not come out of the pink egg.

- When Tubby hatched, the blue egg still hadn't opened.

- Wizzy came out of the yellow egg, he wasn't the last.

Here's the question . . .

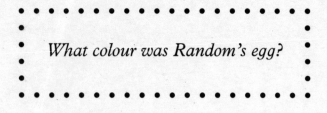

What colour was Random's egg?

Psst! If you need a hint, follow this line . . .

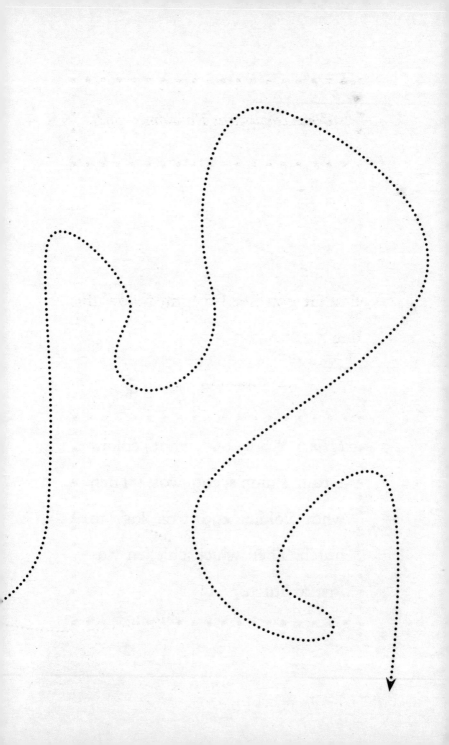

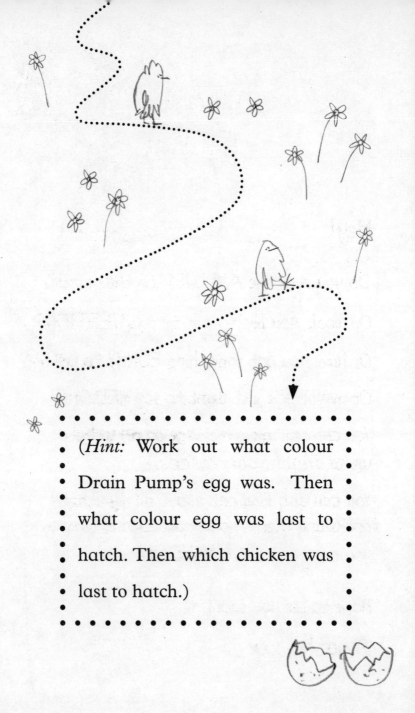

(*Hint:* Work out what colour Drain Pump's egg was. Then what colour egg was last to hatch. Then which chicken was last to hatch.)

Hey!

Do you need the ANSWER to the puzzle?

Or would you like to ask me a QUESTION?

Or have you got something FUNNY to tell me?

Or maybe you just want to say HELLO!!!

You can send me a message on my website
www.agathaparrot.co.uk

You can also find out about all my other
books and there's some quizzes and games
you can print out WAHOO!

Hope to see you soon!

Agatha xxx

Want to read more about ME?
Well, you can! Look out for

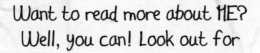

and the Odd Street Ghost

It was a dark and stormy night and someone
or SOMETHING was ringing the bell in the
school clock tower! It got worse when we
saw a horrible face glowing in the window
EEEKY FREAK! But there's no such thing
as ghosts . . . or is there?

There was only one way to find out.
We all spent a night in the school hall
keeping watch, and that's when things
got even stranger . . . WOOOO!

Agatha Parrot